CORTLAND

A PALMER SISTERS NOVEL 4

KAYT MILLER

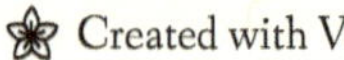 Created with Vellum

*To all of my girlfriends who keep me laughing and sane
(well, sort of).
&
To my mom, the strongest person I know.*

CONTENTS

PROLOGUE

Cortland

I THOUGHT I'd be nervous on my wedding day, but I'm excited as hell. You'd think my family would be all over me about meeting a girl and marrying her two months later, but they haven't been. Not even my mother, who is ordinarily wound tighter than a two-dollar watch, has given me a hard time. No, I think even Emily Ashbury has a lady-crush on my bride-to-be.

Who wouldn't? Polly-Anna Phillips doesn't mince words. She's as real as you can get. It was sure as hell refreshing for me to see, except for the fact that the stubborn woman wouldn't give me a chance. Not for a long-ass time. And damn, I tried to get her attention! She finally agreed, but it was a struggle for nearly a month.

You probably want a little background on all of this before I delve into how I wooed and won the woman of my dreams.

It all started when my big brother, Charles, fell head over

heels for Sadie Palmer. It happened in less than a week. I was shocked because Charles Ashbury is a fuddy-duddy, to put it nicely. Don't get me wrong, the man is probably my best friend. I've looked up to him my entire life. He was the perfect big brother. As a kid, I never felt like I was in the way or a burden to him when I wanted to go wherever he was going, which was all the time. So, when he came to me the second night of our Ashbury family cruise aboard the Queen Margaret and told me that he'd found "the one," I wanted to laugh in his face. That was, until I really looked at him. He was serious. Totally no bull-shit, serious.

Not surprisingly, Charles didn't back down, and I watched him work his ass off for five days straight in hot pursuit of one Sadie Palmer, née Rachel Montgomery—her alter-ego on her cruise vacation. Not only that, after Sadie left him in her cabin without a word, he made it his mission to track her down. Two months later, he finally found her out in the boonies of northern Arizona. A mere bakery owner.

Long story short—I know, *too late*—he discovered she was pregnant with *his* kid the day he finally found her again. Now, this is the part that's all Charles Ashbury. Any other man would have heard the words, "I'm pregnant and you're the father," turned on his heel, marched out the door, and hopped on the family jet on his way back to Boston without another thought. But not Charles. He loved Sadie at first sight—a notion I never put much stock in. It's what fairy tales are made of. But I watched the two of them together on the cruise, and then again recently at a family meeting in Page, Arizona, where we learned that my brother is going to be a baby daddy.

I, for one, am thrilled at the idea of having a niece or nephew. The Ashburys have needed something to liven them up for a long time. A little munchkin is just what the doctor ordered. (Ha! Charles is a doctor. Get it?) Seriously, though, my family is boring. The only bright spot in my entire family is my gran, Laura. She's a fucking stitch—always has a smart-ass comment spewing from of her mouth. I adore her.

Now that you've got a little backstory, I can tell you how I met and wooed Polly-Anna Joyce Phillips. Sure, that name is quite a mouthful, but so is my girl. She's delectable. Gorgeous, blonde, curves for days, and a body made for sin. Picture Lana Turner plus Jayne Mansfield merged into one. What? You don't know them? Google them and you'll see. Gran Laura is always watching those old-time movies.

Anyway, the day I walked into Sadie Cakes Bakery and saw her standing there, I knew. My heart started beating so hard at the sight of the blonde bombshell, I thought it was going to burst out of my chest. I stopped breathing for a full minute. Sweat started to gather at my hairline, my palms began to itch, and I *knew*. Hell, she hadn't even seen me yet. When her baby-blues spotted me, she scowled. She fucking scowled. That's when I realized... this girl was more than drop-dead gorgeous. She was special.

Just about every other woman I've ever met has made a move on me. Having the last name Ashbury hasn't hurt, but even women who have no idea who I am fall at my feet. Now, sure, I'm a little vain. Okay, *a lot* vain. If you looked like me, you'd be a little self-centered too. I'm six foot two and fit. I work out nearly every day, usually doing something with a point to it, like kickboxing, biking outside, or my favorite, playing hockey. Along with my rock-hard abs, I've got light brown hair that's styled to perfection, hazel eyes, a wicked smile, and two dimples that drive the ladies crazy.

So, yeah, when Polly gave me that sassy expression and then blew me off, it took me by surprise. Maybe it's the sass that got me interested in the first place. Whatever it was, I decided, then and there, that I would do whatever I could to make her mine, starting with her name. The second I saw the name *Polly* on the name badge pinned to her blue-and-white striped Sadie Cakes Bakery apron, I immediately broke out into song.

"*Well, hello, Polly!*" Sure, I used the title song of the old movie, *Hello, Dolly!* as my inspiration. So what? It's one of Laura's faves. I've seen it at least ten times. I thought I was clever. It was the perfect icebreaker. But what did the love of my life give me for the effort? An eye roll. That's right. A goddamn eye roll.

'S all right. No problem. I knew I could regroup. I still had game. All I had to do was make a plan. I was good at that. I'm a lawyer, for fuck's sake. I know how to win. And at that moment, I was more determined than ever, muttering to myself, "And win I shall."

CHAPTER ONE

POLLY
  Two months earlier.

YEAH, I saw him––the hottie that just walked into the bakery. My eyes were drawn to him. Of course they were—he's gorgeous. But the thing is, I've done gorgeous before and it never works out. Not for me, anyway. I'm drawn to those guys like flies to a picnic. Or maybe that's ants to a picnic. Either way, they're my kryptonite. I see them, start to salivate and slobber all over myself, and can barely speak to them.

Now don't get this wrong. I'm *not* a novice or a virgin. Far from it. No, I've been around the block. I've dated plenty of attractive men just like that guy, but I'm done with that. (Okay. Not exactly like that. Confession. Cortland Ashbury is a cut above any guy I've ever seen. The first sight of him made my body feel alive. Charged.) But I'm done with that. Kaput. I'm over the good-looking guys. I need to find myself an old man with a paunch and a bald spot who'll appreciate all that is me.

And there is a lot of me: big ass, big tits, and big thighs. It's how I'm built—just like all the other women in my family. It's my lineage.

Men seem to like that about me, at first. In my experience, men like Cortland are enamored with the idea of the Jayne Mansfield type; Jayne Mansfield with extra padding. The thing is, as soon as they sleep with me once or twice, they're done.

I've accepted my fate. If I end up alone, I'll get myself artificially inseminated when I turn thirty and I'll be fine. No worries.

Turning around to face him, I'm about to ask how I can help him when he opens his mouth. "Well, hello, Polly!" he sings. Yes, that's what I said. He *sang* it, like in that old Barbra Streisand movie.

I'm stunned. I remain silent, thinking that maybe he'd keep going with the song but, sadly, he doesn't. It was sort of funny. No matter, it deserved an eye roll so that's what I gave him before saying, "Hello. Welcome to Sadie Cakes. How can I help you?"

"Marry me. Today."

Great. He's one of those. "No." Short and sweet. Stepping over to the glass cases that house Sadie's treats, I ask, "Would you like some cupcakes?"

He's still smiling at me like a fool. *What is up with this guy?* Maybe he's mentally unstable.

"I'll take a half-dozen assorted cupcakes." He pauses. "And your phone number."

"No." I sigh. "You can have the cupcakes, though."

"Fine. No problem. Cupcakes it is." He winks. "I'll just have to keep trying. Perhaps Sadie will help me out."

"No." She'd better not.

Boxing up six cupcakes, I tell him his total. He hands me a

black American Express card and I roll my eyes again, but he can't see me this time.

Handing him his receipt and a pen, I place the box of his cupcakes into a bag and walk around the counter to hand it to him. "Thank you for shopping at Sadie Cakes."

When he reaches for the bag, our fingers touch, and damn it, a sizzle courses down my arm.

No.

No. No. No.

I won't have it. I won't be attracted to this guy. My heart can't take it. I've already mentally prepared myself for artificial insemination in three or four years. I've accepted it. I'm just not the kind of woman men want to keep. Especially men like this one. It's just the way it is.

I watch him walk out the door in his fancy jeans that were probably made just for him because who can find jeans that fit like that? Rich people, that's who. Couple that with the white tee that was probably $250, but with a couple of holes to make it seem like it was five bucks.

Picking up the pen and his receipt, I stare down at the signature. It's signed Cortland Ashbury in a fairly nice script. Shit. His last name is Ashbury? No doubt he's related to Charlie. A brother? I stare at something else he scribbled down the side of his credit card slip: *Call me, Polly.* 555-332-9801.

Cue eye roll *numéro trois*. I shove the receipt into the drawer.

"No."

CHAPTER TWO

Cortland

STEPPING out of the bakery into the warm Arizona sunshine, I ask myself, "What do you get a woman who deserves everything?"

Sliding into my rental car, I push the start button and contemplate that question. I reach over to the bag holding the box of cupcakes I intend to share with Laura and Mom. But the second I bite into one, I moan so loud I scan around to make sure no one heard me through the car window.

"Fuck. So good." This one is a chocolate cupcake filled with creamy chocolate and topped with white icing, and after that? Drizzled with more chocolate.

I sip from the water bottle I've got nestled in my cup holder as I reach for cupcake *numéro deux*. This one is a yellow cupcake. I taste honey and something else. A spice. Rosemary? "Fuck." I moan again. I've never had anything like it.

It's so damn good, I practically swallow it whole. I glance

back at the door of the bakery and smile. "I bet Polly knows a thing or two about baking." What is it about a woman who looks like sin, but you know she's got everything else going for her too? I need to do whatever I can to get her attention. I'd like to get my brother involved with this, but he's out of town right now. No, I can do this. I just need to come up with a plan. First, the name. "Ha!" I laugh, reaching for a third cupcake, another yellow one. "Mm, lemon." It's topped with white fluff, like a meringue, and more lemon.

"Focus, Cort," I say with my mouth full of sweetness. I've got it. I'll call it Operation: Win Polly.

As I finish the lemon treat, I lay my head back on the head-rest and brainstorm on what my first move should be. "She works in a bakery so she probably wouldn't want sweets," I say aloud.

Well, chocolates could be nice. But not just *any* chocolates. Pulling the phone from my back pocket, I search my contacts. I know the perfect thing. I find the international number and dial. Peeking at my dashboard clock, I calculate the time difference. It's about 6:30 P.M. Swiss time. I hope they're still in, because I *must* have DeLafée of Switzerland expedite an order of the Gold Chocolate box. It's $330 and contains eight chocolates made with edible 24-karat gold flakes, each applied by hand. It also comes with a gold coin from the Swiss national bank that was minted between 1910 and 1920, all packaged in a silk-draped wooden box. It's something special. I know she'll love it. Then, I'll be *in*.

As I wait for someone to answer, I reach for cupcake number four, topped with crumbled bacon. I bite into it and get a little faint. Maple and bacon are the perfect combination. "How is this not in every damn bakery in the world?"

"Hallo," says a woman in a thick German accent.

"Hallo. Sprichst du Englisch?" I know a little German but not enough to pull this off.

"Yes, sir. How may I help you?"

I recite my order and ask for it to be rushed. I pay the bill using my black AMEX, and that's it. *Perfect.* Commence Operation: Win Polly!

Once that's done, I reach for the fifth of six cupcakes and bite into a cupcake delivered from the heavens. Three words. Chocolate. Covered. Cherry. "Jesus. So fucking good." I'm going to gain fifty pounds pursuing my girl. Totally worth it. You'd think that many cupcakes would be too much for one man, but I'm an Ashbury. We're made of stronger stuff than that. We were built to eat cake. Lots and lots of cake.

CHAPTER THREE

"WHAT'S THAT? Did you order something?" Sadie asks as she stocks one of our glass cases with one of her crazy cupcake recipes.

I think this one is called Banoffee Pie. Banana and toffee. I shiver at the thought. She knows what she's doing, but I've got to stick with my vanilla-vanilla combination. For someone my size, it's probably a surprise that I'm this picky about sweets, but hey, it's just the way it is.

An international parcel with the recipient listed as *The beautiful Polly c/o Sadie Cakes Bakery* was just delivered to the bakery a few minutes ago.

"No. I don't know. I haven't opened it up yet."

"Well, open it."

"Cool your jets, woman. I'm doing it." I tear open the box, pull the flaps open, and stare down at a small box wrapped in cloth. "Hm."

"What is it?"

I reach in and pull it out, handing it to Sadie. On the side of the box is printed *Cioccolato al latte con nocciole.* Whatever the fuck that is.

"Ooh, it's chocolate with hazelnuts. Who's it from?"

She can read that shit? "No idea." In the box, there's a small ivory-colored card. Picking it up, I read, "Sweets for the Sweet." I rolled my eyes.

"Does it say who it's from?"

"It's just signed with the letter C." I look at my bestie. "Maybe it's for you. I don't know a C person. But Charles would totally send you something like this."

"But it's addressed to you."

I shrug. "Well, let's see what we've got here." I grab the scissors and cut away the cloth wrap. Opening it, I see eight little balls wrapped in gold paper that form a circle surrounding a gold coin in a small plastic container. "Fancy," I mutter.

Handing one to Sadie, I take another, unwrap it, and pop it in my mouth. It only takes me a second to realize that there's paper wadded inside the thing. I quickly spit out my chocolate into my hand and see more gold paper half-chewed along with the melting chocolate. "What the fuck?" I mutter.

Sadie reaches out, picks up some of the gold, and slides it into her mouth.

"That was in my mouth, woman."

She shrugs. "It's edible gold leaf."

"Uh-huh." I slide the box over to her. "Have at it."

"Really? I'm pretty sure this is probably expensive. Ooh, and there's a gold coin in here."

I reach out and grab that. "I'll take this. You take the choco-late. Put it on some cupcakes or something. You know I don't like weird shit in my mouth."

"That's what she said." Sadie laughs. "True. Okay. I'll whip up something new and top them with these candies. It can be our special today."

"Cool." I shrug. "I like the cut of your jib, woman."

Sadie laughs as she heads back into the kitchen while I break down the box that icky candy came in and continue to set up for the rush of customers that will inevitably start about ten minutes from now.

CHAPTER FOUR

Cortland

I STEP into the bakery bright and early. So, like ten or so. I know the chocolates were delivered because I received a text notification to that effect this morning. The bell above the door chimes, drawing her attention to me. She glimpses me over her shoulder. Our eyes meet. Then, inexplicably, she moves through the swinging doors to the back. Away from me. Out of my sight. Saying just loud enough, "Sadie. You've got company."

Refusing to let it bother me, I step up to the case to see what they've got on offer today. I'm not going to lie—I've got a sweet tooth. The first day I was here, I may have told Polly I was going to share the cupcakes with others, but that's not what happened. I ate all six sitting in my car.

Bending down, I glance at all the options available to me just as the doors to the back swing open again. Sadie walks out and approaches me.

"Cort. What's up?"

I love how casual she is. It's so refreshing. "I just thought I'd come in and visit my girl while also stockpiling some goodies. Two birds and all that."

"I'm not your girl."

"I know." I smirk.

"Oh. Hm." Sadie turns her head toward the back but then turns to face me. "Good luck with that."

"Hm," I mumble, mimicking her. Bending down again, I scan the case. When I come across a cupcake with a golden icing, I move closer and squint. Pointing at the tray holding seven cupcakes, I ask, "Are those topped with Swiss chocolates?"

"Hey, yeah. How d'you...?" She stops talking. Staring instead. "Oh. Shit. You sent those?"

Standing up to my full height, I arch my brow. "I did. I had them expedited from Switzerland."

"Oh." Sadie giggles. "That...." Her giggles turn into a full-blown laugh. "That was s-sweet."

I should probably stomp out of here all angry and such, but right this minute I've got to know what's so damn funny. "Why are you laughing?"

"Polly is...." She glances back to the swinging doors that lead to some really delicious smells. "She's very vanilla."

"Vanilla?"

"Yeah. She doesn't like 'weird' treats. Her words. Not mine. She won't try anything that isn't plain and simple."

"So, expensive candy?"

"There was 'gold shit' in them." Sadie starts to laugh again, and it's getting really annoying.

"Got it. Simple is best."

"Well, let's not go that far." Sadie is wiping tears from below her eyes. "Polly's complicated."

"I heard that," Polly shouts from the back room.

"You are," Sadie shouts back. "I'd go so far as to call her high maintenance."

"Am not!" she shouts. "I just like what I like."

It's Sadie's turn to arch her brow. "See?" she whispers.

"I can still hear you, bitch."

It's my turn to engage. "So, no chocolates?" I say loud enough for her to hear me.

"Hershey's."

Sadie nods knowingly.

"What about dinner?"

"No, thanks." Polly answers without even thinking about it.

"Fine." I release a breath. "Give me a dozen assorted." I need to regroup, and while I do that, I'm going to eat the fuck out of my feelings the minute I walk out of here.

CHAPTER FIVE

POLLY

"WELCOME TO SADIE CAKES. How can I...?" Shit. It's him again.

"My love," he coos. "I searched high and low for the perfect flower. One that reminded me of you." Reaching out, Cortland hands me a bouquet of tiny pink roses. The tiniest roses I've ever seen. "These are wild roses."

"Tiny roses? *I* remind you of a tiny rose?" Yeah, right.

"Light pink roses symbolize admiration. That, and your skin is pale pink, and your lips are tipped in this shade." He points to one rose that's slightly darker than the rest.

"Hmm, interesting."

I take the flowers and lay them on the back counter.

"You don't like them?" I stare at his face, and I'm a little surprised to see he appears somewhat defeated.

"They're nice. I'll put them in water as soon as I take care of you."

"Ooh, I like the sound of that."

I arch my brow because that's just... ick.

"I mean, as in we take care of each other."

I arch the other brow.

"Forever. After we're married. It's what people do when they commit to one another." He runs his hands through his perfectly coiffed hair. "Wow, this is hard."

That's what she said. Okay, I didn't say that out loud, but it's on the tip of my tongue.

"What can I get you today, Cortland?"

"Ah, she knows my name." He winks. "At least we're on a first-name basis, dearest Polly."

Doing my damnedest to contain the eye roll that's yearning to be free, I point to the case. "What'll it be, tiger?"

He chuckles, and it's warm and buttery.

"Very well." He steps over to the case. "I'll try any new cupcake flavor you've got plus two of those chocolate croissants."

He's so focused on his selections that he doesn't see Sadie approach. "Whatcha getting, Cort?"

"Ah, sis. I'm going to let my girl choose the other items in my box. I'd like a box of a dozen, please."

"Fine," I say with a sigh. I quickly fill up a bakery box and set it on the counter. "Anything else?"

"Dinner. Have dinner with me?"

"No." I reach for a bag. "Anything else?"

"Sadie. My future sister. Help me out."

I turn to my bestie and give her the evil eye. She knows I'm not going to touch whatever Cortland Ashbury is dishing out.

"I'll do my best, Cort. No promises."

Traitor.

"IT DOESN'T SEEM like he's giving up," Sadie says the next day.

Cortland just left the shop a few minutes ago, leaving behind a basket full of Hershey's candies and a note. Well, not a note. A poem. He wrote me a poem. Damn him to hell.

"What's the note say?" my nosy friend asks, peeking over my shoulder.

"It's a poem." With a sigh, I read:

Your voice is as sweet as the treats you dispense...
    My heart beats like a drum and the feeling is intense...
    When I think of true beauty, I see your face...
    All things considered, you're worth the chase.

"Wow," Sadie says, blinking at me.

"I know."

"What're you going to do?"

I shrug. "Nothing. He's leaving, right?"

"He's coming back."

"What? For how long?" I shove the poem into my apron pocket.

"Charlie thinks he's going to stay here for a while. Maybe you two—"

I interrupt her. "I just can't, Sades. I know it's going to end up biting me in the ass. I just can't right now."

Sadie moves closer and wraps her arm over my shoulder. "If this had all happened a year ago, hell, six months ago, I'd have been on board with you rebuffing him. But now...?" She squeezes my upper arm. "I say you've got to go for it. You just never know."

I do. I know. He'll get one look at me completely naked and that'll be it. I should probably stop wearing Spanx. It gives people the impression that I've got real curves.

Setting the basket of goodies on the back counter, I smile at my friend. Throwing her a bone, I say, "I'll think about it."

"Have dinner with him. What's it going to hurt?"

My heart.

I shrug. "Maybe when he comes back." If he comes back.

"That's a start." Sadie smiles at me. "Okay, now I'm going to go puke. Back in a minute."

I laugh, because, well, it's funny. My pregnant friend has had it rough.

CHAPTER SIX

Cortland

I'M BACK. No, not in Boston. I'm back in Page, Arizona, after spending just over four days out east packing up enough things to stay in Page for the foreseeable future. I wasn't lying to Laura; I love it here. While it's plenty warm, northern Arizona has a more varied climate than in Phoenix or even Sedona. Hell, it even snows here occasionally. I suspect it'll be hotter than hell in midsummer, but so is Boston. No, I think I'm going to like it here just fine.

"Cortland?" My grandmother's voice comes from somewhere in her huge Page home.

"In here, Laura." She likes to be called Laura, says it makes her feel younger. "In the kitchen," I say louder. I'm sitting at her enormous kitchen table drinking a cup of coffee and planning my next attack.

I look up just as Laura walks into the kitchen with her newest employee, Thomas, in tow. I've yet to hear the story about how he came to work for her, but I'm sure it's a good one. He seems cool. Not a surprise. Laura has a good sense about people.

"Well, there you are, my dear," she says.

"Morning." I nod at Thomas as he moves further into the kitchen.

"Good morning, Mr. Ashbury."

"Cortland. Please. Or Cort."

"Alrighty," Thomas says as he begins work on something in the kitchen. Hopefully, more coffee. I drank the last bit.

"Why are you up so early?" Laura says as she receives a small glass of water and her morning vitamins and supplements.

Checking my Baume & Mercier Clifton Club watch, I note the time. Nine o'clock. It is early, for me. Sort of pathetic, actually. I believe I heard Sadie mention that she and Polly get to the bakery at 4:00. A.M. Shaking that off, I answer Gran. "Planning."

"Planning?" She chuckles. "You going to take over the world?"

"Nope. Attempting to win the love of my life."

"Oh? So, you mean plotting." She chuckles again. "Who's the lucky girl?"

"Polly."

"Sadie's friend?" Laura's brow arches.

"The one and only." I smile brightly.

"So..." Laura pauses when Thomas brings over a steaming cup of coffee and sets it down in front of her. "She's the one?"

"Yep."

"Tell me."

"Tell you what?"

"How did you know she was *the one*?"

You probably think it's odd that I'm chatting with my gran like this, but Laura Ashbury is one of my closest confidantes.

I've always told her things I've never told anyone else, so the fact she's asking me such personal questions is nothing new.

"Well, the second I saw her my heart started beating hard." So did my dick, but I'm not about to tell Laura that part. "I began to sweat. I couldn't catch my breath. I thought I was going to pass out."

Laura chortles. "Well, it certainly sounds like you had a physiological response to her. Did she react the same way?"

I scoff. "No. She won't give me the time of day."

"No?" Laura smirks. "Smart girl."

"What?" I slap the table. "Why would you say that, Gran? I've been doing all the romantic stuff."

"Like?"

"Sending her expensive candy." *That she hated.* "Taking her flowers." I add rather shyly, "Writing poetry."

"Well done. You wrote it yourself, correct? You didn't just find it on the interweb and claim it as your own?"

"Hell no, Laura. My words. All of them." Jesus. I'm not a complete moron. I know how to write a damn good poem.

"And she hasn't swooned yet?" I half expect Laura to laugh but she doesn't. Her expression is soft, sincere.

"No. Not yet. That's why I'm trying to figure out what to try next."

"Oh, dearest...." She sighs. "You know how much I adore you."

I nod. She does. Hell, who doesn't? Oh, right, Polly doesn't.

"I'm going to say this, but I don't mean it as a criticism."

Shit. "Okay."

"Well, sometimes you come across as rather cavalier."

"Cavalier?"

"You know... cocky."

"Cocky," I mumble, because I know this.

"Yes. Cocky. So, my first bit of advice would be to be your-self. Be the Cortland that we all know and love."

I nod, because it's the only way to keep this going.

"Have you tried really talking to her? Have you asked her about herself?"

"Of course." I pause. "Well. No. I haven't had the opportu-nity. She won't give me the damn time of day."

With an eyebrow arched, she asks, "Have you been giving her winks and flirty one-liners?"

"Well. Uh." I have to think back at the things I've said to her. They have been short snippets. I mean, the stubborn woman won't give me a chance to talk. "I've asked her to dinner every time I've seen her, and she turns me down flat."

"Have you enlisted the help of Sadie? Your brother?"

"I asked Sadie. She said she'd try."

"Well, why don't you see if Charles would like to double date. You'll need to get Sadie on board if Polly is resistant. Plus, isn't there a big wedding coming up?"

"I think Charles said something about Sadie's sister getting married."

"Have you secured an invitation?"

"No. But I will." I'm sure Polly will be there. At least I assume. Only one way to find out. I jot down *Call Charles*. "Good idea. I'll get to work." I stand from the table, empty cup in hand. "If you think of anything else, text me."

"Will do, honey. Good luck. She's quite a looker."

Yes, she is.

"You'll make pretty babies."

I turn to Gran. I feel my eyes grow round and my mouth spread out into the biggest smile I've ever created—so wide it hurts. "We will, Gran. We'll make beautiful babies. I wonder how many she wants to have?" *What if she doesn't want kids? Then what?*

"Holy shit," says Laura as she spits out her sip of coffee. "You're really in love."

"I'm really in love."

"I'll be damned," Laura says with a big smile. "Then I'll do what I can from my end, Cortland."

"Thanks, Gran."

With her in my corner, how can I fail?

CHAPTER SEVEN

POLLY

"HOLD THE DOOR FOR ME, would ya, Sadie?" I've got the first and largest layer of Lainie's wedding cake in my arms, and it needs to go into the back of Sadie's Ford Focus wagon.

"Got it. Hang on," Sadie says, passing by me. Holding the door open, she moves out of the way of the door, using her arm to keep it propped open.

"Now the tailgate on your shaggin' wagon."

Sadie laughs at my term of endearment for her 2003 hunk of junk we use for bakery deliveries. Hey, don't get me wrong. I'm jealous of her 2003 hunk of junk. Trust me. I watch as she opens the back end. I bend at the waist to slide the large round cake base into the back. "Now the rest."

I carry the heavy cake layers, since my bestie is pregnant, while she grabs the other, smaller, lightweight elements needed to tier the cake. Not to mention the special cake topper. A bride and groom on the back of a motorcycle. Sadie's gift and surprise for her sister and husband-to-be. *To be* later today.

"Let's make sure we didn't forget anything." We scan the bakery, Sadie's office, and make sure everything is locked up tight.

"Meet you there," Sadie says, hopping behind the wheel of her Ford.

"Yep. I'm following you."

Sadie and I are meeting at the reception hall first to set up the cake. Then we'll race to the church so Sadie can get dressed for the ceremony. I'm already dressed for the day in one of my favorite dresses. I'm not in the wedding party, so I don't need to match the rest of the girls, but I won't stick out like a sore thumb either since Lainie's colors are deep jewel tones and charcoal. My dress is a pretty plum color, and I've dressed it up with a pair of silver-hued strappy stilettos. The dress is chiffon, so it's soft and floaty. The top has a deep v-neck and flutter sleeves. It's tight at my natural waist, but then it floats out like a cloud, hitting me right at the middle of my knee. I seriously love this dress. I've worn it for pretty much every wedding I've been invited to since I bought it two years ago, plus on a couple of dates. A couple of bad dates. I've changed it up with sweaters, scarves, and jewelry enough times in an attempt to disguise it. Not today, though. Well, I grabbed a cardigan in case it gets chilly. What? It could happen. It's September, after all.

At the church, I linger at the back, waiting for one of the ushers to walk me to a seat. If I had to guess, I'd say all the ushers come from Gustafson Custom Motorcycles. They have that rough-and-tough bearded biker thing going on. I like the style, sure, but I tend to go for the more clean-cut yuppie types.

When I hear the church door open and see light flood into the entry, I turn. Of course, it's him. Cortland. I watch as he scans the room, passing over me for a second, but then his eyes jerk back to me. He gasps. I hear it. I watch him lift his palm and rest it over his heart, then a smile slides across his lips.

I'd like to smile or at least smirk, because I know this dress is a good one for my body type. I school my expression though. I'm sort of interested to know what he'll do now that we're no longer at the bakery. We're on neutral ground now.

"Be still my heart," he says as he approaches me. "Honest to God, Polly." He scans me up and down and, for some reason, it gives me a chill. The good kind. Then he says quietly, "You take my breath away, Polly-Anna."

Shit. How'd he discover my middle name? Well, one of them.

"You look nice too." And he does. He really does in his dark suit. I can't tell in this dim interior if it's dark gray, black, or blue but I can tell how well it fits him.

"Thank you." He smiles at me rather shyly.

Who is this guy?

"I didn't realize you were invited."

"Well," he says, leaning in a little closer, "I had to secure an invite from Charles and Sadie."

"Had to?"

He gives me a shy smile. "I think it's the only way I'm going to get you to dinner."

Wait. He scored an invitation to have dinner with me? "Well, there are a lot of people here." Like a shit-ton. "It's doubtful we'll even be sitting at the same table."

"Never doubt the tenacity of a man when he sees what he wants."

Oh. "Oh."

"Yeah." He leans closer. "Oh."

Our intimate little talk is interrupted when one of the ushers asks, "Are you ready, ma'am?"

Ugh, I hate being called ma'am. And by an usher who's at

least ten years older than I am.

"Shall we?" Cortland places his hand on my lower back, gently nudging me toward the entrance to the main part of the church.

I should really think of some way to get away from him. Maybe Sadie needs help? Or Lainie? I bet someone needs me.

"Don't even think about it," Cortland says, his breath warm on my ear. "I can tell you're about to make a run for it, sunshine."

I snort. *Sunshine?* I'm the least sunny person in this room. "Fine." I let him guide me to a seat on the bride's side of the church. As we scoot down the pew, I notice Cortland is seated next to someone who works with Lainie's ex-husband at the bank. And next to him, Lewis, Lainie's ex.

What the hell is he doing here?

My body is jostled when someone bumps into my arm. I turn to see a gorgeous guy. A big, gorgeous guy I've never seen before in my life. Even seated, I can tell he's tall with short reddish hair. God, I love redheads. He leans down. In a deep, sexy voice says, "Well, hello."

I begin to raise my hand to introduce myself when a warm palm slides over my shoulder. That same hand nudges me to my left, closer to Cortland. Cortland leans around me and smiles at the hottie on my right. With his hand out, he says, "Cortland Ashbury." He smiles at me, "And this is my girl, Polly."

"Sig Engel," he says in a deep, gruff voice.

"Sig? That's a great name," I say with a giggle.

"Cortland's nice too, though, right, princess?"

"Sure." I don't take my eyes off Sig. "How do you know Lainie?"

"Oh, is she the bride?"

"She is." I titter. "I can't believe I've never met you before."

Leaning closer, Sig whispers, "I'm a new friend of the

groom's family."

"A new friend?" I try to ask because I think this mystery man has a story to tell, but I'm interrupted.

"Welp!" says Cortland, suddenly not letting me hear Sig's story. The jerk. "The groom's side is over there. You should go. There are rules to follow. We wouldn't want to upset the bride." Cortland chuckles, but it's forced.

"Don't be silly. There are no *rules*," I say, smiling at Sig.

Sig scans the other half of the church. "Actually, I see another friend over there. I'd better get to my side." He leans down and smiles at me. "See you later?"

"Sure."

I hear a growl next to me, so I quickly turn to face Cortland. "*What* is your problem?"

"My problem?" he whisper-hisses. "I've been doing my damnedest to get your attention. To go to dinner. Hell, to get you to just talk to me, and what do you do? You flirt with the first asshole you see when we're *obviously together*. Who does that?"

"We're not *obviously together*," I snap. "We're sitting next to each other."

"Princess," Cortland says with another growl, "this is more than merely sitting together, and you know it."

No. I don't. I really don't. "I know you want there to be more, but for the life of me I can't figure out why." Shit. *I said that out loud.*

Shit. Shit. Shit.

Cortland's eyes suddenly appear as though they're smoldering. "Sweetheart." He reaches out, placing my hand in his. "You're the most beautiful woman I've ever seen in my life."

I roll my eyes. Such a line.

"Please don't roll your eyes at me when I'm trying to say something important."

Instead of rolling my eyes, I just give him the evil eye. "Fine. Tell me. What do you see in me? What's so damn fascinating about *me?*"

"Everything," he says, sounding sort of breathless. "Your beauty, yes. But your sass, your frankness, the obvious love and care you have for your friends. Your passion for your work."

I don't get it. He comes across so cocky. "Well, sure." I laugh. "I guess I am pretty awesome."

"Polly. Awesome doesn't even begin to cover it."

Damn this guy.

"The day I walked into the bakery, I thought I was having a heart attack. My heart beat so hard, my pulse rate increased, and my palms started to sweat. I've never, ever, had a reaction like that." He chuckles, but it sounds forced. "Then you blew me off."

I'm staring into his pretty hazel eyes. I say quietly, "You don't really know me." And guys that get to know me don't seem to like what they see, so....

"Let me *get* to know you. Give me a chance, Polly."

Before I can answer, movement in front of me catches my eye, and Keeton Gustafson steps out in front of the church with the minister. My God, that man is gorgeous in jeans and a T-shirt. Seeing him in a dark gray tuxedo is making my ovaries explode.

When the music begins to play, I watch as one by one the Palmer sisters step down the aisle with their wedding partner. First is Molly, Keeton's sister, walking with a man I don't recognize. I suspect he's from Keeton's shop. Sadie is next, walking next to a woman. Deb, Keeton's ex-wife.

I smile at the sight of the two of them. It's so cool Keeton and Lainie are both close to his ex. I know she adores Lainie too.

I'm tempted to lean forward and glare at Lewis, but I resist.

The next through the door is Keely. She's walking with another bearded dude. She's got a big smile on her face, especially when she sees Nick Martelli sitting two rows ahead of me. Hell, me too. The man is sizzling hot. Agatha is walking with her fiancé, Ian. Ian and Keeton have become good friends.

The last couple to walk down the aisle are Violet and Keeton's little brother, Eric. My goodness. Violet is absolutely stunning in her floor-length gown. They are each wearing the same style of dress, but they chose different colors. I'd say Violet's dress is the perfect shade of, well, violet.

I watch Vi's face and can't help getting a little teary-eyed. She's beaming as she moves toward the rest of the bridal party. But the interesting part is what Eric is doing. He's gazing at our sweet Violet with such adoration. There's a gentleness in his expression too. "Oh, shit." My eyes burn with tears. The bridesmaids aren't supposed to make me cry, damn it.

"Babe?" Cortland leans closer. "You okay? Can I get you anything?"

I shake my head. "No. Happy tears," I choke out.

From the corner of my eye, I watch Cortland reach into his inner pocket, pulling out a white cloth. A handkerchief. A real one. Like the one my grandfather used to carry around. "Here, beautiful."

I adored my grandfather.

"Thank you." I take the hanky and dab at the corners of my eyes just as the traditional "Bridal Chorus" begins to play. We all stand as Lainie Palmer, in a stunning ivory ball gown, begins to walk down the aisle on her father's arm.

"Oh, shit." I press the handkerchief to my eyes as the waterworks start up in earnest now. "She's b-beautiful."

"She is," Cortland whispers in my ear. "But she doesn't hold a candle to you, my love."

Fuck. I'm in trouble.

CHAPTER EIGHT

Cortland

"HEY, LITTLE BROTHER."

I don't even bother moving from my slumped position at the banquet table at Lainie and Keeton Gustafson's reception.

"Why so glum?" Charles claps my shoulder as he sits down next to me. "Come on, Cort. This isn't like you. It's a party. You're usually the life of said party."

I shrug. "She won't give me the time of day," I say, sounding like the saddest fucker who ever lived.

"Polly's working. She and Sadie have been cutting cake for a good thirty minutes."

Yeah, but that's not all. "Yeah, well, she's danced several times with other men. I've asked her multiple times, but she refuses to dance with me."

"Don't give up."

I turn to stare at my brother. I can see from his expression he means well. "What am I doing wrong?"

"Nothing." He runs his fingers through his hair. "I shouldn't say this...."

I perk up. "What?"

"Sadie told me...."

"What? Spit it out, dude."

"Please don't get me in trouble. I'll tell you what she told me, but you've got to keep it to your damn self."

I nod.

"And don't fucking tell Laura."

"What is it?" God, I hope it's the secret to Polly's heart.

Charles scans the room. "Let's step outside."

Wow, this shit must be good. I follow Charles out the door to a massive balcony that overlooks a golf course. Country club reception. Interesting. When he finally stops walking, we're far enough away from the party that no one will hear a word.

"Let me say all of this first."

I nod. I'm fucking ready.

"Polly has bad taste in men."

Uh... "And?"

"What'd I say?"

To let him say all this first. I close my mouth.

"She finds you attractive, but she's afraid to do anything else because—"

"Because she has terrible taste in men? What does that have to do with me?" I say angrily. "I'm—"

Charles holds up his palm. "Let me finish."

"Fine."

"Sadie says you're doing the right thing. Chipping away at her resolve."

"So, the gifts?"

"According to Sadie, the gifts are good."

I haven't stopped sending her things. Even while I was back in Boston, I had things delivered. For example, one day I had her favorite lunch delivered to the bakery from the Italian restaurant across the street. (Thank you for the tip, Sadie.) Another day, the small spa in town delivered a gift basket filled with lotions and other girly stuff.

On the last day I was away, the same spa gave her *and* Sadie a massage in the back of the bakery. According to Sadie, Polly smiled the rest of the day. I guess that's something.

I have something for her tonight too. Something really special. That is, if she lets me anywhere near her. I plan to escort her home. No, I don't mean *that*. I'm not going to rush intimacy with my girl. I want her to want me too.

"Shit." My shoulders slump.

"What?" asks my big brother.

"What if she doesn't want me?"

"Are you going to let me finish?"

I nod.

"Just be yourself, Cort. Not the cocky one who picks women up at clubs. Be the one I helped raise. My brother and friend, Cortland."

"I am." I'm doing that. Or am I? "Fine. I'll do my best."

"Go find her. Be her date. Don't just sit back here and mope. You should be by her side." He stops talking.

Finally.

I wait for more.

"Go!" he shouts with a laugh. "Go get her."

Hell, yeah. I turn on my heel and march back into the reception to win my girl.

CHAPTER NINE

POLLY

HE'S EVERYWHERE. At some point in the evening, he appeared at my side and he hasn't left. Well, except to get me a fresh drink, or a piece of white cake, or another piece of white cake. Other than that, he hasn't left my side. He's asked me to dance multiple times, but I haven't accepted yet. I don't know why. The music is fun and lively. Hell, I danced with several guys from Keeton's shop before Cortland became my hunky shadow. I should just do it. Dance with him.

Why am I so damn scared? Me? The fierce Polly-Anna Joyce Phillips. I'm strong enough to endure Cortland Ashbury. I can survive him. I must.

Setting my drink down on a nearby table, I turn to Cortland. "Come on, stud. Dance with me."

Damn, his smile. It's something. His teeth are perfect, as are his lips. He seems happy right now. "As you wish."

He leads me to the dance floor, and I'm ready to cut the rug with some sweet 70s disco, when the fast song ends and a slow song begins. Damn it.

Before I know it, Cortland's arm is wrapped around my waist, his big palm on my lower back. He takes my hand, intertwines our fingers, and brings it up to his chest. Staring down at me, his face has changed. He's happy but there's more to it. There's a calmness to his expression. "Finally," he whispers into my ear. "I've wanted to hold you since the second I saw you."

Oh.

"NO MORE GIFTS, CORTLAND," I say, holding a large gift wrapped in beautiful pink foil wrapping. The ribbon around it is like spun silk. "You don't need to buy me gifts."

We're sitting outside my apartment building in Cortland's car. I let him drive me home. Sure, my car was there, but I'd been drinking, and apparently, Cortland hadn't been.

"We'll see." He smiles. "Just open it."

Gingerly, I pull the ribbon away from the package. Setting that aside, I tear away the paper. I'm not one who usually hangs on to wrapping paper, but this stuff is amazing. Flipping over the gift, I pull open the back. Cortland takes the wrapping paper out from under the gift, allowing me to turn it back over in my lap.

"It's a..."

"Star map."

"A star map?" What's a star map?

"It's a star map of the night sky."

I turn to him. I swear he's vibrating with excitement. I want to laugh, but I'm afraid I'll hurt him. "A star map."

"It's literally a map of the stars and sky on the date, time, and location of the day we met."

I blink. "Oh."

Oh, oh, oh.

Shit.

Below the round map of the sky reads: *The Moment We Met.*

Shit.

Never in my life have I ever gotten something so... sweet, romantic. "Cortland." My nose burns and my eyes water.

Shit.

"Do you like it?"

Oh, shit. I love it so much. So much it terrifies me. "Cortland," I say, choking up. "It's the most amazing gift anyone has ever given me." Honestly. The best. I smile even though tears have begun to slide down my cheeks. Time for some honesty. "I'm scared."

"I know." His hand reaches over to rest on my face and his thumb wipes away a tear. "I was too."

"You aren't anymore?"

"Nope." His head moves from side to side. "Not anymore."

"Do you want to come upstairs?"

"Polly. This isn't about sex. I'm not trying to seduce you."

I know. "I believe you." And I do. I think I believed him the second he made his intentions clear. "Come upstairs."

"If you're sure."

"Positive."

CHAPTER TEN

Cortland

FINALLY. Polly is finally willing to give me a shot. Why is that so terrifying? Probably because I'm concerned that she'll find me lacking. Not just in bed but everywhere else. What if I'm not what she wants? What if she pictures herself with someone else?

Shit.

I can't worry about it. I've got to be myself and show her how much I adore her.

With her hand in mine, I walk next to her up the one of steps to her apartment. "My place...." She pauses. "It's probably not what you're used to."

I lift her hand as I bend down to kiss it. "I'm here with you. I don't care where that is."

"Okay," she says, sounding unconvinced.

Pulling her hand away, she unlocks her door. Pushing it open, I motion for her to step inside first. I follow her inside and wait for her to turn on a light. Once that happens, I smile. Her place is small, for sure. My bedroom in Boston is twice this size, but it's quirky and colorful. Polly has splashes of color all over the place from the walls, to throw pillows, to the mixed and matched rugs on the floor. Smiling, I say, "I like it. It's happy." And it is. It's got a joyous quality to it.

"It *is* my happy place," Polly replies.

"I can see why."

"Would you like a drink?" she asks quickly.

"Water would be good."

Opening her fridge, Polly pulls out a small bottle of water. I take it in hand, twisting off the lid. Taking a long pull, I move into her living room area. I call it an "area" because it's combined with a small eating nook. There's one large bookcase filled with books along one wall and a small flat-screen television resting on top of an old wooden trunk that's painted in bright primary colors.

Following my line of sight, she points to the trunk. "That was my grandfather's trunk." She laughs. "He let us paint it when we were kids. I'm pretty sure we ruined it."

"I love it." I could see it in *our* home in a place of prominence.

Moving around the room, I see many framed photos, old and new. Some people I recognize from here in Page and others from the wedding earlier. "Is this you?" I point to a photo of a girl in her teens.

"Ugh, yes." She laughs. "Stupid braces."

"You were beautiful then too." I mean it. "I bet if we'd gone to school together, I'd have had a crush on you then." More than a crush.

She makes a noise that doesn't sound like she agrees.

"What?"

"No one liked me."

"*I* would have."

"No, Cortland. I was the biggest girl in my class. You wouldn't have liked me."

I turn to her, walking deliberately. "Please don't presume to know what I would have thought back then. I knew the second I saw you, you were mine. I'm positive it would have been the same thing then."

She rolls her eyes. I both love and hate the eye rolls. Right now, however, I don't like them. Wrapping my arms around her, I pull her closer to me. Without another word, I slowly lean down until our lips are millimeters apart. "This is it, Polly."

With her slight nod, I press our lips together. Holding still for a second or two, I bring my hand up to slide into the back of her hair. Moving my lips over hers, back and forth, I slide my tongue over her plump bottom lip and moan.

Let me in.

Her mouth opens like she heard my thoughts, her tongue peeking out enough for ours to touch. I can't get close enough to her even though her breasts are against my chest, my legs pressed to hers. No doubt she notices my arousal between us. "Polly," I whisper as I move my mouth down the side of her neck to her collarbone. "Sweet, beautiful Polly."

My hands are yearning to touch the rest of her, but I won't until I know she wants me to.

When she pulls away, I'm disappointed. That is, until she takes my hand and pulls me down a short hallway. We both remain silent as she leads me into a small bedroom that holds only a double bed and a dresser. A small closet, overflowing with clothes, is partly open on my left. Next to that is a small window propped open by several books. There's a slight breeze coming in but not enough. It's hot. And not because of the Arizona weather. No, it's hot because Polly is sitting on her bed, bending down to remove her silver sandals. All the while her eyes are on me. "You going to stand there all night?" she asks me huskily.

Hell, no. I quickly remove my jacket, tossing it into a corner. Then my tie, belt, shoes, socks and finally my shirt. Standing in only my slacks, I wait as Polly stands. Turning her back, she peeks at me over her shoulder. Damn, it's sexy. "Unzip me?"

Fuck, yes. It's what I'm thinking, but I remain cool. Stepping closer to her, I wrap my arm around her middle, leaning down so I can kiss her exposed neck. "We don't have to do this tonight."

"Unzip me."

I move back so I can grasp her zipper, slowly bringing it down until it falls from her shoulders, then slides down to the floor. Stepping out of her dress, she turns. I stare down at her and smile. She's wearing one of those stupid undergarments that keep all of her curves hostage.

"This is me, Cortland."

"No, that's a medieval torture device," I say, pointing to the nude-colored spandex.

"It's necessary," she whispers. Pulling the strap from her shoulder, she wiggles and wrangles the damn thing down below her breasts. I'd like to stop her right there because, holy hell, her breasts are magnificent, but I can tell just from her expression that this moment is significant. It means something to her.

Rolling the elastic down to her waist, she stops to take a deep breath. I'd like to help, but I'm not sure if I should. Turning us around, I'm able to sit on the bed with her between my legs. I take her hands and push them to the side. My turn. Sliding my fingers inside the stupid girdle, I give it one big push until it moves down over her hips to her knees.

Pushing it to the floor, she finally kicks it away, leaving her in only panties. I scan her from her feet to the hands resting on her hips. Then up past her breasts to her face. Her expression reads defiant, her eyes squinting ever so slightly. Is this a challenge?

"Beautiful."

"What?" She throws her hands in the air. It makes her amazing tits bounce. "You can't be serious. You just watched me undress. You saw me, no, you helped me take off my Spanx." She pushes one of my shoulders. "Who does that?

"I do." Placing my hands on her hips, I pull her closer. "First, stop wearing that shit. You don't need it. Your body is fucking amazing."

She scoffs. She doesn't believe me? Time to show her. Unbuttoning my pants, I push the zipper down. Lifting my hips, I lower my pants and boxer briefs so she can see the evidence.

"Holy shit, Cortland," she says with awe.

Yeah, I'm the entire package. "This," I point to my cock, "is what you do to me. No matter what you're wearing." I gaze down at her. "And especially what you're *not* wearing."

"I give up," she says, sounding defeated.

"On me?"

"No. I give up trying to convince you I'm not good enough."

Wrapping her up in my arms, I pull her down toward me so we're lying on the bed facing one another. "I'm the one who's not good enough. I'm an asshole on most days. But, Polly," I kiss her cheek, "I won't be to you. I promise. I'll do whatever I can to make you happy."

Leaning closer, Polly kisses my lips. "Show me."

I waste no time kicking my pants off the rest of the way. Nudging her up to the center of the bed, I begin by kissing her. My mouth on hers makes my body come alive. I sweep my tongue in to tangle with hers, then move down her neck, licking and nibbling along her collarbone. Pressing my face between her breasts, I take in her scent. Perfect. Placing one hand on each breast, I bring them to the center so I can lap at them both, back and forth.

"Cortland," she moans.

"Marry me," I whisper. I mean it. But she says nothing in response.

Sucking on her hard nipple, I pinch and squeeze her other breast. I swear I could play here for hours. Polly's hand moves into my hair, pulling and tugging on the longer strands on the top of my head. I love that. I take it as a sign to keep moving, so down I go. Kissing her ribs, then down further to her soft belly. I lick around her belly button and nudge my nose further down, taking in the scent of her arousal.

"Marry me, Polly," I say into her flesh.

She still says nothing.

As I'm about to reach the motherland, Polly presses her legs together tightly.

"What's wrong?" I ask, panicked. Damn, I'm so fucking hard I could blow any second. Please don't tell me she's stopping this.

"Not tonight."

What? What's not tonight? "What?"

"I want you inside me."

So, no oral tonight. For now, anyway. Moving up her body, I let my hands stroke her soft-as-silk skin. "Your skin is perfect."

"There's a lot of it," she mumbles.

I stop what I'm doing. Moving up to my knees, I peer down at her. Her face is flushed, which is good, but I watch in slow motion as her hands move to cover herself. "Enough," I say, rather angrily.

"Enough of what?" she snaps.

"Enough with the comments about yourself."

"I'm not. I didn't."

"You did." I'm scowling at her, and if it weren't for the little light coming from her window, I'm not sure she could see it. "What do I need to do to prove to you that I think you're the most fucking beautiful woman I've ever seen?"

She scoffs again, and that's it. I'm pissed. "Do you want a spanking?"

"Huh?" she says, surprised, but then giggles. "Maybe?"

"Not tonight." I quickly press myself against her so she can feel what she's doing to me. I kiss her lips, softly at first, while I slide my cock through her wetness. I want to be deep, deep inside her, but not yet. Finding her clit with my tip, I slowly move back and forth. Shit. I'm not going to last like this.

"Inside," Polly pants. "Please."

Reaching down, I use my palm to open her up wider. Seeing her open up to me like a flower is more than I can take. I move to her entrance and slowly press in. Jesus. The feeling. Euphoric. I'm seeing stars floating around my head. Staring up at her, she's not speaking either. Pushing all the way in, I stop. I have to. "Polly," I whisper. "Marry me."

I've asked her three times tonight and I've meant it each time. But now that I'm inside her, and she's holding me so tightly, I know I'm where I'm supposed to be.

"Marry me."

I pull away and quickly press back in.

"Yes." Polly's voice is soft and breathless. "Yes."

I stop moving again. "Yes?"

"Yes. Now, don't stop. I need you."

Holy fuck. "Yes." She said yes.

CHAPTER ELEVEN

POLLY

WHAT HAVE I DONE?

Those are the first thoughts this morning as I spy the clock that reads 3:30. That's my usual wake-up time, but the bakery is closed today because of the wedding yesterday. So, here I am, wide awake in my bed, with a large man wrapped around me like a vine.

I blink to clear my head about last night. I wasn't drunk, so I remember everything from the reception, the car ride home, and Cortland in my bed. The gift. Oh, the damn gift from Cortland. And the sex. The man is a machine. He took it slow the first time, proposing multiple times until I finally said yes. After that, the sex was fun, playful, experimental. At least it was for me. I'm a missionary kind of girl. I think it flatters my body, you know, lying on my back. At least it makes my stomach appear flat. Flatter, anyway. But Cortland isn't a missionary kind of guy, apparently. Well, the first time was missionary. After that, he showed me what I've been missing.

On top of his skills in the sack, he seems to like to please me. I stopped counting the number of orgasms he gave me after four. Sighing, I think back to the parts I enjoyed the most. I attempt to roll over so I can slide out of bed, but the big palm on my hip slides around, holding me in place.

"Where're you going, princess?"

"I have to use the restroom."

"Fine." His palm moves back, squeezing my bottom once as it goes. "Hurry back, fiancée."

Shit. Fiancée?

I wasn't lying; I needed to use the restroom, but I didn't return to bed. Instead, I wrapped myself in the robe I had hanging on the bathroom door and tiptoed to my kitchen to make a cup of tea. As my electric pot warms up, I take a moment to look out the window. It's still dark and will be for another two and a half hours. I should go back to bed.

When the teapot is done, I pour the steaming liquid over a teabag. As I'm about to take my first sip, I feel an arm wrap around my middle.

"I thought you were coming back to bed," Cortland says as he moves my hair away from the back of my neck. His lips are soft at the base of my neck and even softer as they move right to that spot below my ear.

I feel his hands next as they slip through the opening in my robe. His palms cup my breasts as his fingers tease my nipples to life. Setting the hot cup down, I lean back into him. I can't help it. The man has magic fingers.

"Come back to bed," he whispers.

"No, Cort." I stop speaking when his right hand begins to slide south. "We need to talk."

Ignoring me, he asks, "Are you wet for me?"

God, yes. I keep that to myself. I'm sort of speechless right now. We *do* need to talk.

When his finger slides through me, the man moans in my ear. "Bend down. Hold on to the counter."

We can talk later.

Oh, Christ on a cracker. I do as he instructs. As I bend, Cortland drags the robe from my shoulders and off until I'm completely nude. I don't know what he's about to do, so I'm startled when I feel his tongue slide through me. "Your pussy is like a pretty pink flower."

I'd roll my eyes, but I can't focus while he uses his tongue and fingers to bring me to another orgasm. I'm a little embarrassed by the speed with which I can let go with him.

Before I know what's happening, Cortland stands, bringing his body over mine. His mouth is on my neck, words are flowing freely, and he slides into me from behind. "So beautiful, Polly."

"God." It feels so good. We didn't do this last night. He's deep. So fucking deep. I grip the countertop while he holds my hips, pumping in hard and fast. I begin to move back and forth against him. It's amazing.

"Play with yourself," Cortland pants. "I'm close." One hand on the countertop, I slide the other down over my clit. My finger brushes his dick as he glides in and out, and Cortland growls. "Do it, honey."

Circling myself, it takes mere seconds to come. While Cortland grunts, I release a long, low moan. When he pulls out, wetness slides down the insides of my legs. We haven't used protection at all. Why I let that happen, I don't know. But we should address it. "Cortland. We haven't been using condoms."

"No, we haven't," he says, standing nude in my kitchen. I watch him pick up my tea and sip. *He likes tea?* I suddenly remember who he is. Cortland Ashbury is rich. *Stupid* rich. And I'm not. I'm a nobody.

What the hell am I doing?

I reach down and pick up my robe, quickly tying it in place. "We need to talk."

Cort arches one brow. "About?" God, he looks so damn smug.

"This!" I shout, pointing back and forth between us.

"You mean *us?*" He's smiling like a fool.

"Yes. Us." I stomp my foot. "There is no us."

"I beg to differ. I proposed. You said yes."

"During sex. It doesn't count during sex. You had me at a disadvantage."

"Ah, I see. So, we're not having sex now." He moves closer, and before I know it, he's on one knee. Naked. On one knee. And I swear his dick is getting hard again. "Marry me."

"No," I say quickly and turn to run to the bathroom, but he's faster than me. Blocking my way, he does it again. On one knee. Naked. And now he is completely hard. Big and hard. "Marry me."

"Cortland," I whine. "This makes no sense."

"I know." His words are soft, quiet. He's no longer looking smug. "I'm not joking. Regarding the condom, I'd never have gone bareback if I didn't think you were it for me. I saw your birth control pills in the bathroom."

"You snooped in my bathroom?" If he'd snooped better, he'd have seen those are expired. I haven't been on the pill in months. I break out like a teen on the pill. Shit.

Crossing my arms beneath my chest, I snap, "I could still be pregnant." I'm not ovulating, so it's doubtful, but he needs to be scared straight right now.

"I hope so."

"What!?" I stomp my foot again. So childish, I know. "We don't even know each other."

"So we'll get to know each other while we're planning the wedding. I already know you prefer white cake."

I roll my eyes so hard it hurts. "Cortland."

From his knees, his hands move to my hips, then around to my ass, pulling me closer. "Let me prove it to you. You've already said yes, so that's a done deal."

"No. I can change my mind."

"I'm a lawyer. Good luck with that."

"You're a lawyer?" Why didn't I know that?

"A good one."

If he's a lawyer, I'm sure his work is out east. This'll get him. "I'm not moving."

"I'm already house hunting, but I'd prefer if you were in on that since it'll be yours too."

"You can't be serious."

"I'm extremely serious. I'm also going to hang my shingle here too."

"You're opening up a business? Here?"

He nods. "I want to be where you are."

He's killing me with all this sweetness. "So, when's the wedding?" I ask sarcastically.

"November 16."

That's only a month away. "In a month?" I screech. "That's not enough time."

"We'll have it at Laura's home. The view is spectacular there, plus the house is large enough for a reception. We already know a great cake decorator. The rest will be easy. How many people would you like to invite?"

I stare down at him while thinking about his question. My mom and brother. I'll have to ask Parker if he'll give me away, since my dad is gone. Oh, crud. I'm going to cry. My dad won't be able to give me away. He died several years ago, but this is the first time I've considered the importance of that. It's a rite of passage. Damn it.

"Baby, what's wrong?" Cortland stands and wraps me in his arms.

"My dad died."

"When?" He looks shocked.

"Three years ago."

"Oh. All right."

"He can't give me away."

"Oh." He rubs my back gently. "I'm sorry."

"My brother can," I say with a sniffle.

"I'm glad to hear that. I'd like to meet him."

"And my mom. You need to meet her. She's awesome."

"What about your grandfather—owner of the trunk."

I sniffle again. "No, everyone is gone."

His hands are caressing me, and my eyes are fluttering; it feels so good.

"At least your mom and brother will be there, right?"

"Yeah." With bells on.

"So, November 16?"

I nod into his bare chest.

"Let's celebrate." Cortland takes me by the hand, leading me back to my bedroom.

I'm not sure I can do it again but by the looks of him, he's raring to go.

"Come along, future wifey." He chuckles. "Let me show you a glimpse of the rest of our lives."

Wifey? The rest of our lives?

Shit. What the hell have I just done? I think I just said yes to Cortland Ashbury. I'm getting married.

CHAPTER TWELVE

POLLY

"OH, my God, Polls. You're getting married today!" shouts my best friend, Sadie.

"I know."

"Aren't you nervous?"

I'm not. Strange, because I'm sort of a nervous person, especially around men. Clarification, good-looking men. But Cortland Ashbury is the exception to that rule. Honestly, the moment I saw his gorgeous, smug-ass face, all I wanted to do was punch him in the nose. God, he's so damn arrogant.

"Twenty minutes, girl. Time to get that dress on."

Ugh, the dress. I nearly gave up the search. I mean, you try finding a plus-size bridal gown at the last minute. It was nearly impossible. That was until Laura, Cortland's grandmother, flew me and my girls to New York City for a combination wedding dress search and bachelorette party two weeks before my big day. *Our* big day. Talk about a blast. Yes, Laura was footing the bill for the entire thing. I didn't like the idea, but she insisted. And who was I to argue? It was her grandson's fault that this thing had to happen *immediately*. Was he afraid I would change my mind? Maybe at first, but not anymore. Sure, I said my first impression of him was that he was the same kind of guy I was always attracted to but honestly, that's not him at all. There's more depth to the man than I ever imagined. Under all that hair gel is a sweet and sexy-as-hell man. Not to mention he is a god in the sack. If I have less than three orgasms, he thinks he's failed.

Holy shit. I found my unicorn.

CHAPTER THIRTEEN

Cortland
The Wedding

I'M speechless as I watch Polly's brother escort the most beautiful woman I've ever seen down the aisle. My girl is beaming, her beauty a beacon for me in her wedding dress—the perfect wedding dress. It's tight in all the right places, but I can see from her expression that she knows how gorgeous she looks. She should. No one has ever looked that good on their wedding day. *No one.*

I feel a tear slide down my cheek, and I should probably be embarrassed, but I'm not. No fucking way. I'm proud to cry as I watch Polly walk into my life forever.

Before she takes my hand, the justice of the peace asks, "Who gives this woman in marriage?"

"Her mother and I do," Polly's brother, Parker, says with tears in his eyes.

I step down from the small stage we've set up and reach for

her hand. With hers in mine, we step back up to begin the ceremony. My eyes are on Polly rather than the officiant.

"Dearly beloved, we are assembled here in the presence of family and friends to celebrate the joining of this man and this woman in the unity of marriage."

"There are no obligations on earth sweeter or more tender than those you are about to assume. There are no vows more solemn than those you are about to make."

"There is no human institution more sacred than that of the home you are about to form. True marriage is the holiest of all earthly relationships. The state of matrimony is based in this deep, invisible union of two souls who seek to find completion in one another. Do you understand this?"

We say together, "We do."

"Will you please face each other and join hands?"

We both turn as I take both of her hands in mine.

"Cortland Alexander Ashbury, will you take this woman, whose hands you hold, choosing her alone to be your wedded wife?"

"I will."

"Will you live with her in the state of true matrimony?"

"I will."

"Do you promise to love, honor, and obey her?"

"I will."

"Will you love her, comfort her through good times and bad, in sickness and in health, honor her at all times, and be faithful to her?"

"I will."

"Polly-Anna Joyce Phillips, will you take this man, whose hands you hold, choosing him alone to be your wedded husband?"

"I will."

"Will you live with him in the state of true matrimony?"

"I will."

"Do you promise to love, honor, and be patient with him?"

"I will promise to love, honor, be patient with him, and talk things over with him before I make up my own damn mind."

The audience laughs at the obvious change of wording. No worries. I'm okay with it. She *is* going to need to be patient with me. And I will obey her. She's my queen.

"Will you love him, comfort him through good times and bad, in sickness and in health, and be faithful to him?"

"I will," she says with a smile that lights up the entire room.

Next, we exchange rings. Mine is a simple yellow gold band, and hers, well, hers is something special. It was Laura's wedding band when she first married my grandfather. It's also yellow gold with small rose-cut diamonds all around the band. She said she wanted a simple ring so she could still wear it to the bakery and not have to worry about it when she has to take it off to work.

I stare down at the ring on her finger, then up to gaze into her eyes. This is it.

With a few final words, the officiant says, "Ladies and gentlemen, I now present to you Mr. and Mrs. Ashbury."

The small group all clap as we continue to look at each other. I'm smiling like an idiot, but her smile is angelic.

"Cortland, you may kiss the bride."

Oh, right. It's official. "Hell, yeah!" I shout at the top of my lungs adding, "Woman, you're mine." Then, I kiss her like I mean it. *With* tongue.

<u>The Palmer Sisters</u>

Lainie

Agatha

Sadie

Cortland

Keely

Violet

Molly

<u>Standalones</u>

The Art of the Game

The Virginia Chronicles

One of a Kind

The Portrait Painter

Game Changer

Bedhead

Coming Soon: FarmBoy

<u>The Flynns</u>

Out of the Blue

Mick'sology

<u>Vested Interest</u>

The Importance of Being Ernie with Bonus Book The Importance of

Being Kennedy's

Quirky Girl

<u>For a complete list of Kayt's books, visit:</u>

Kayt's Website: www.kaytmiller.com

ACKNOWLEDGMENTS

Thank you to Olivia at Hot Tree Editing for editing this book
from start to finish.

And an extra special thank you to Becky at Hot Tree
Promotions for your advice, expertise, and your positivity.

And for my beta readers.
Thank you so much for your time and feedback!

How did it all start? Well, I love reading and one day I was searching for a book. A book about a certain type of woman and a specific kind of man and I couldn't find it so, I wrote it. I called it Game Changer and it couldn't have been a more appropriate title. It changed my life in many ways. While my real job is teaching young people, my fun job is conjuring up characters and situations to write about.

My goal, as a writer, is to write stories that relate to all of us, to make readers laugh and maybe cry sometimes. I hope my readers can escape into a fantasy, one that's actually possible. Sure, some of the stories could be dubbed "Insta-love" stories but that's okay. I fell in love with my husband pretty damn fast and with my daughter the second I saw her. So, it's a thing, I swear.

Please Follow Me on these social media sites. Following on BookBub to learn about special book deals.

I love hearing from you!

facebook.com/authorkaytmiller

twitter.com/kaytmiller1

instagram.com/kaytmiller1

bookbub.com/profile/kayt-miller

The Palmer Sisters Cover Designs
by
Colleen Galligan
galligancolleen@gmail.com

Colleen,
Thank you for all of your hard work
and creativity on the new covers!
I love them! KM

Thank you so much for reading Polly and Cortland's story! When I start a story, it begins with an outline, notes, and lots of crazy thoughts running through my head. When I actually start writing, the characters take over, leading me through the story like they're holding my hand—guiding me. The process is exciting and cathartic. With that said, I hope you enjoy the story.

If you did, please go to my website, www.kaytmiller.com, and join my newsletter so you can be the first to know what's coming up next. And...

And remember...Please, leave a review!

Thank you!

Chapter 1

Keely

"Fluckity-fluck-fluck."

I must have been too busy singing along with my favorite song to pay attention to my driving because I just noticed the flashing lights in my rearview mirror. The loud whine of a police siren is barely audible over the music. I wasn't speeding. Was I? Well, maybe I *was* driving just a tad over the limit. My little 2003 Honda Civic is surprisingly zippy. But no worries, I've dodged a ticket or five in the past.

"I'm sure I can get out of this too."

Yeah, I know I'm talking to myself in the car, but it helps to keep me focused on my goal. I know I can do this. I've discovered that all I have to do is flutter my lashes and show my dimple and, bam, I get a warning. Works. Every. Time. Watch and learn, *biatches*.

Looking into my rearview mirror, I watch a man, clad in

black police gear, stride to the driver's side of my car. "Well, hello Officer Hottie," I whisper to myself.

I lose sight of him for a second, so I roll down my window and spot him in my side mirror. As he approaches, I'm struck by the sheer size of him. He's tall. I can even tell that from my vantage point in my little car. I should add that he's not just tall, he's big. And I mean BIG. His muscles have muscles.

"License, registration, and proof of insurance please, ma'am."

Ma'am? I'm twenty-five. Ma'am isn't supposed to start until I'm old. Like forty.

"Ma'am. I haven't got all day."

Well, shit. His voice is deep and smooth like sweet, sweet honey. I can imagine the ways he could use that voice.

My attention turns away from thoughts of his sexy tone of voice to the torso in my driver's side window. I scan up his dark uniform noting how perfectly pressed the thing looks. Then up to the shiny golden badge on his meaty pectoral that reads: *Page Arizona - To Protect and Serve.*

Mr. Police Officer has dark hair but I can't see it very well due to his police hat. He's got olive skin and five o'clock shadow on his chin, which is remarkable since it's only noon. I watch as it tenses like he's gritting his teeth. His lips are stretched thin. Stress. I bet his job is stressful. When my eyes meet his, I only see myself. No, I don't mean that like some romantic sonnet or some shit. I mean I literally see myself in his super-reflective cop aviator sunglasses. My eyes move down to see a very strong nose. There's a little bump on the bridge which means it's probably been broken before. Not surprising for a cop. My guess is he's been in a tussle or two. My eyes move lower. By the looks of his flaring nostrils, I don't think he's happy.

"Ma'am? Did you hear what I said? License, registration, and proof of insurance. Now."

Damn, he sure is demanding.

"I'm sorry Officer, but what did I do?" I flutter my eyelashes and ever so subtly push my shoulders back, so my chest sticks out just a tiny bit. I say tiny bit because it's all I've got.

With a very heavy sigh, he pulls his glasses off his face, revealing golden brown eyes and long dark lashes. They're gorgeous. Why do men always get those long lashes? It's so not fair. "Excessive speed and your taillight is out."

Oops. I knew about the taillight but those are hard to fix. First I'd have to YouTube it, then I'd have to try to buy the replacement bulb and who knows where you buy one for a car as old as Bluebell. We're talking days of work right there and let's not forget what a pain it is to undo the plastic cover and the thing-a-ma-jig to replace the stupid light. Ugh, I'm exhausted just thinking about it. Apparently this guy doesn't know how hard it is or he wouldn't be giving me such grief.

So, I do what I've gotta do. In as shocked a voice as I can muster, I say, "My tail light is out?"

Ooh, that was good. I even convinced myself I was shocked at the news.

"Yes, ma'am."

Doing my best to look unassuming and cute, I place my palm on my chest like a southern belle fanning herself and flutter my lashes again. I have the urge to say. 'well fiddle-dee-dee' but instead, in a breathy Marilyn Monroe kind of voice, I say, "Officer, I had no idea."

I watch his eyes roll. That's not a good sign. He's not falling for my cuteness and charm. Strange. It's worked in the past.

"Ma'am. I'm only going to ask one more time. License, regis-tration, and proof of insurance."

Flustered now, I grab my purse from the seat beside me and proceed to dump the entire contents of the bag on the seat and floor of the passenger side. "Shit." I mutter.

"Today, ma'am."

I give him a little dirty look but say sweetly, "Oh, sure. Let me find them."

Then I hear his voice rumble even louder as he asks me, "Do you know how fast you were going?"

I turn my head toward him and smile. Bam, there it is, my dimple. "Um, the speed limit?" See, how adorable was that response? I sounded a little dumb but still cute.

"I don't have all day, ma'am."

"Um, okay. Here's my license." I hand him my photo ID and smile again. He's going to love that picture. I took a good one this time, thank goodness. My last license picture made me look like a serial killer. No joke. Ask my sister Violet.

He sighs, heavily. Evidently he's got more important things to do. "Now I need your registration and proof of insurance. Sometime today would be nice."

Impatient much?

I'm at a loss for words but I speak anyway. "Right. I'm getting it. Hold your horses."

"Excuse me?"

"I said, hold your horses, geesh."

I abruptly reach over the seat to open my glove box. I must have startled him because I hear my door being wrenched open.

"Step out of the car, ma'am."

"What?"

"Step. Out. Of. The. Car. Was that clear enough for you?"

"Well, yeah, but you don't have to be a jerk." Forget I ever considered him good-looking. Now he's Officer Not-So-Hot-Anymore. He stands with his left hand on the doorframe and his right hand on his weapon. I quickly unbuckle my seatbelt and exit my car. I stand up to my full height and realize that I'm looking right at the shiny badge that's pinned to his front chest pocket. His name, MARTELLI, is forged into the shiny metal shield, but it should say JERKFACE instead. I snort again, aloud. Will I ever learn?

I turn to face my driver's side door but that's not good enough. "Move to the back of the vehicle, please. Out of the road. Hands on the trunk."

"Yes, officer Bossypants."

Silence.

"Ma'am, keep your comments to yourself. I don't want to have to take you to the station. Please place your hands on your vehicle and spread your legs."

"I'm getting frisked?" I squeak. "Is that really necessary?"

"Please stop talking, ma'am."

The pat down startles me. I wasn't expecting to get frisked today—or ever, really. I'm a good girl. I'm a kindergarten teacher! Who does this guy think he is? I did nothing wrong! But Officer Meaney says nothing.

He begins the pat down at my sides and his hands move down quickly to my hips and up the inside of my legs. A shiver runs through me that's probably inappropriate under the circumstances. Sue me. I can't help it. The man is cranky *and* hot. A lethal combination.

"You can step back into your car. I'll need your registration and proof of insurance for the ticket."

"Serious? You're going to give me a ticket?"

"Serious. Yes, ma'am. You were traveling forty-five miles per hour in a school zone."

"B-b-but, it's spring break! Schools aren't even in session! I should know." My sputtering, exasperated responses are not helping me at all. I can't believe I've used all of my usual charms and I'm still getting a freaking ticket. I mean I've tried flashing my dimple, fluttering my eyelashes, and I may have stuck my miniscule boobies out so far I sprained something. And let's not forget the wink.

"Registration, insurance, ma'am. Don't make me ask you again."

I reach into my glove box and grab every paper and booklet in there. I dig through and find what he needs.

He takes my papers and license back to his squad car and I wait. And wait. And I wait some more. How long does it take someone to write a damn speeding ticket? After what seems like hours but was probably more like twenty minutes, Officer A-hole returns with my papers and my lovely parting gift—a $267.40 speeding ticket.

"Two hundred and sixty dollars!?" I squeak. I don't have that kind of money sitting around. I'll have to sell a kidney or something.

"Two sixty-seven." He starts to turn, but stops to add, "And forty cents." Tapping the brim of his hat, he smirks. "Have a good day ma'am," he says as he walks—no, saunters—back to his police car. Before he slips inside, he turns back to me again. "Slow down and get that taillight fixed."

I'm practically sputtering, but I don't have a reply. I'm in shock. I mean...what a nightmare. My cuteness powers must be dimming. Without those, what's left? Just a boring old 'ma'am' of a kindergarten teacher.